T0196086

Dancing Butterfly

ALICIA SAGE

WESTBOW
PRESS®
A DIVISION OF THOMAS NELSON
& ZONDERVAN

WestBow Press books may be ordered through booksellers or by contacting:

WestBow Press
A Division of Thomas Nelson & Zondervan
1663 Liberty Drive
Bloomington, IN 47403
www.westbowpress.com
1 (866) 928-1240

Interior Image Credit: Alicia Sage

ISBN: 978-1-9736-8973-7 (sc)
ISBN: 978-1-9736-8974-4 (e)

Library of Congress Control Number: 2020910352

Print information available on the last page.

WestBow Press rev. date: 06/04/2020

Dedication

A Love story; Written for my Children, about Myself.
Dedicated to my Father, the man who named me
Dancing Butterfly when I was only fifteen
years old.

Gentle silence, absolute peacefulness,
unconditional love, surrounded by a deep calm sea of blackness.
Her body weightless, her breath endless, her heart soaring free.

The caterpillar opens her eyes, catches her breath and lets it go. "Why?" she wonders. "Why must I awake from such a dream? Why must I be allowed to feel such things as if I am completely surrounded? So real I could reach out and touch the stars."

As she longed to be back in her dream, the caterpillar felt changes taking place inside of her. Changes she could not understand, yet so strong that it felt like something pulling on her heart. She sat thinking. It felt as if she was supposed to be on a journey. Like great things were supposed to happen and she was meant to be part of them.

5

As time passed, caterpillar was still pondering on the struggle she felt inside herself. Soon it began to get dark. The stars started to appear one at a time, until they spread across the night sky. Like diamonds scattered across a sea of blackness, she thought.

As she gazes out at the huge night sky surrounding her, counting the stars, she sees the moon. Stunningly beautiful, He shines bright, she thought. A sense of calm came over her and she could feel his love, like hands reaching down to comfort her; she could feel him. She loved the moon. As she watched him out among the stars, she longed to dance with him.

"What would it be like to be utterly free?" she wondered. "To be surrounded by the vastness of space, to feel so small; yet larger than life." She wanted to dance with the moon so badly, even if only just once.

Looking up to him, she said, "You and me, we have a date. From which you may return me late." And blows him a gentle kiss, as if to promise him of her return. Caterpillar goes into her cocoon beneath the starry sky; to await her fate. She must begin her journey and stop the struggle inside herself.

The moon watched over her cocoon night after night, waiting for her return. One night the moon grew so tired that he drifted off to sleep. When he awoke, the ground was covered in a thick white blanket of snow. He could no longer see her cocoon.

Panicked and sad that he neglected to protect her, he searched and searched. Though he couldn't find it, he did not give up hope. She had promised to return, and he wanted to be there when she did. The moon watched and waited. Night after night he waited.

After many months had passed, winter began to turn to spring, and the snow began to melt. He was overwhelmed with joy, only to find that when the snow was gone, so was her cocoon.

The moon was so sad that he began to cry. Like rain his tears fell, hitting the ground where her cocoon had once been. But just when it seemed all hope was lost, something amazing happened. The morning sun came and warmed the ground where the moon's tears had fallen. And in that moment, a tiny, delicate flower had sprouted. Something amazing and new to replace the sorrow of something lost.

When the moon saw the tiny sprout where her cocoon had once been, his hope came back. He decided to love and protect the tiny flower just as he had loved her. Night after night he watched over, loved, and protected that flower. And as he did, it grew. Growing taller and stronger as each day and night passed.

Each day the morning sun warmed and comforted the flower. Each night the moon loved and protected the flower. On the fifteenth night, beneath the starry sky, another miracle happened. The flower began to bloom.

The delicate, fragile petals slowly and gently opened up. He could see something in the center. Just as hands gently holding something precious, the flower was holding a beautiful butterfly. And the moon knew it was her, his caterpillar! She had returned just as she had promised.

As she spread her wings, for a moment she and the flower were one. Feeling for the first time a new sense of herself. Almost as if she had been reborn. She had completed her journey and returned transformed. She catches her breath and lets it go. Just like that, she took flight to dance with her moon!

Her body weightless, her breath endless, her heart soaring free! Lost in the vastness of space, she felt so small; yet larger than life. In the gentle silence, the absolute peacefulness, she could feel his unconditional love. And as they danced surrounded by a deep calm sea of blackness. . .

He named her Dancing Butterfly.

The End

Just when the caterpillar thought the world had given up on her,
she turned into a butterfly.
Unknown

In loving memory of my Grampa,
Charles "Ed" Gardner.

About the Author

Alicia Sage is an American writer, born and raised in Idaho. She describes her writing as nothing more than words simply flowing from a pencil. She began writing as an adolescent to cope with life. Dancing Butterfly is her third work and second short story. Her previous works are, A Thousand Burning Thoughts and Lilly and the Prince. Alicia describes her short stories as children's fairy tales, written with deep purpose and morals. Though her poetry is what started it all and is what she hopes can help others see light in their own situations.

Message from the Author

I am still just a girl in this world; on a journey endless. I watch fate unfold before me; as I've dreamt it and felt it. I have been frightened by dreams and feelings all my life, knowing now they have a purpose. As I catch my breath and let it go, I say to the world,

Listen to your heart. Follow your dreams. Reach out and grab those stars. No matter how small you feel, you are larger than life.

With every breath in my body I believe miracles happen. We shall return to a place unknown, weightless and peaceful. Loved unconditionally, we can fly free, so love yourself and one another.

Instructions:

Use this next section to demonstrate your talent and skills.
Color the Illustration outlines yourself.
You can't go wrong, when you follow your heart!

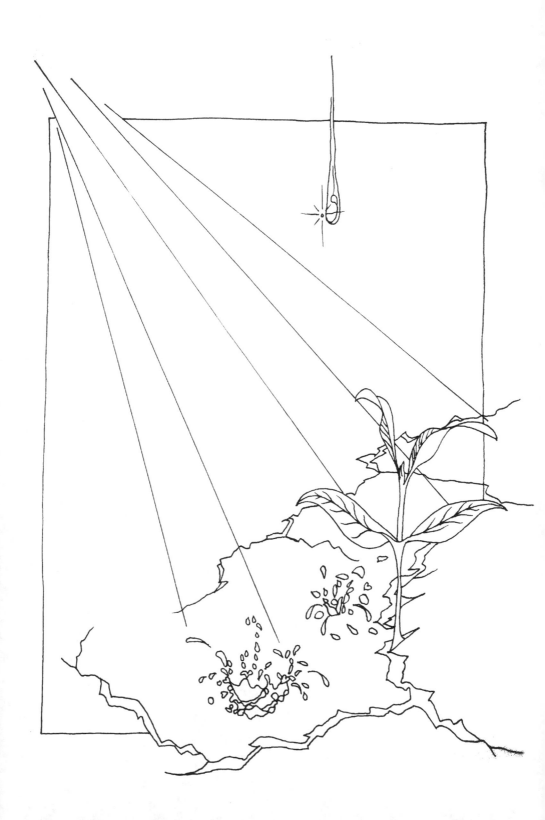

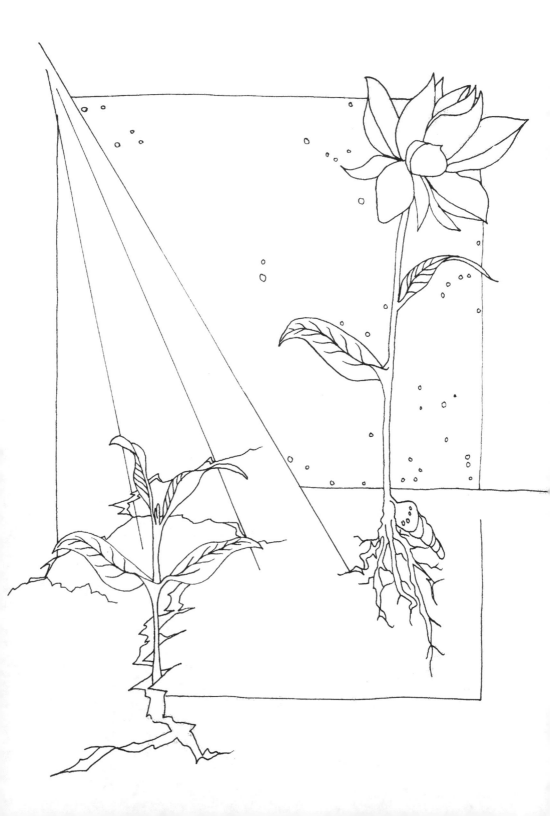

Love, Always, Alicia & Sage

Printed in the United States
By Bookmasters